Artesian Press

THE HAUNTED BEACH HOUSE

SUSANNAH BRIN

Artesian Press

P.O. Box 355 Buena Park, CA 90621

Take Ten Books
Chillers

Alien Encounter	1-58659-051-0
Audio Cassette	1-58659-056-1
Audio CD	1-58659-295-5
Ghost in the Desert	1-58659-052-9
Audio Cassette	1-58659-057-X
Audio CD	1-58659-296-3
The Haunted Beach House	**1-58659-053-7**
Audio Cassette	**1-58659-058-8**
Audio CD	**1-58659-297-1**
Trapped in the Sixties	1-58659-054-5
Audio Cassette	1-58659-059-6
Audio CD	1-58659-298-X
The Water Witch	1-58659-055-3
Audio Cassette	1-58659-060-X
Audio CD	1-58659-299-8

Other Take Ten Themes:
Mystery•Sports•Adventure•Thrillers
Fantasy•Horror•Romance•Disaster

Project Editor: Molly Mraz
Illustrator: Fujiko
Graphic Design: Tony Amaro
©2001 Artesian Press

www.artesianpress.com

 *Artesian Press* ISBN 1-58659-053-7

T1 P2 P1

CONTENTS

Chapter 1 5

Chapter 2 14

Chapter 3 20

Chapter 4 28

Chapter 5 37

Chapter 6 45

Chapter 7 50

Chapter 8 56

Chapter 1

Hudson Miller heard the blast of a car horn. "Oh, hold your horses," he grumbled as he scooped up his duffel bag and laptop computer. Feeling like a condemned man, he gave his room one last look around.

Hudson sighed as he walked down the stairs. He didn't want to go, but there was just no getting out of it. Not unless he wanted to spend his summer detailing new cars at his father's dealership—which he didn't. Working for his Aunt Dot *had* to be the lesser of the two evils.

He closed the door behind him and ran toward the old blue pickup parked at the curb. Opening the passenger door, he nodded at Jose Durango.

Jose was dressed in his usual white T-shirt, jeans, and work boots. Hudson glanced down at his own black polo shirt, beige pants, and sneakers. *I should have worn jeans*, he thought to himself. Then he shrugged. It didn't matter. He had work clothes in his bag. He tossed his bag into the back and folded his tall, lanky frame into the passenger seat. With all the tools and bags of nails in the way, he could barely make a place for himself.

"Don't they have a lumberyard down at the coast?" he grumbled. Hudson was a little annoyed at the clutter on the seat and floor. Where were his legs and feet supposed to go?

"Sorry about that. Dot hit a sale at Andrews Lumber," Jose laughed.

"I should have known. Good old Aunt Dot can't pass up a sale. I've got a drawer full of green and red socks that were half price after Christmas."

"You, too?" Jose laughed. He pulled up the leg of his jeans, showing off socks patterned with reindeer. Then he started the pickup and headed down the street.

Hudson shook his head. It was just like Jose to actually *wear* the socks. *We're the same age*, he thought, *but as different as night and day. I'd rather go barefoot any day than wear those silly-looking socks!*

As the pickup nosed out onto the freeway, Hudson groaned. "I told you we should have left after the morning commute. Now we'll be stuck in traffic for hours."

"Don't worry. Traffic will thin out once we get to the coast highway. Besides—what's the hurry? We've got all summer to fix up the beach house," said Jose.

Shaking his head, Hudson reached for his laptop. It wasn't that he didn't *like* Jose. He did. He just didn't like the idea of spending the whole summer fixing up an old house.

He and Jose had been friends for three years—since they were both fifteen. Aunt Dot had found Jose shivering in the freezing rain on a street corner in Portland. As was her habit, she'd taken the boy under her wing. She'd done the same thing with Hudson when his mother had died. Even though he still had his father, Aunt Dot had felt it was her duty to mother him. So here he was—roped into one of her many projects. Aunt Dot liked buying up old houses almost as much as she liked saving people.

Hudson flipped the switch on his laptop and called up a new database program he'd been developing. Jose glanced over at the computer and sighed. *There will be no talking to him now*, he thought. Hudson was like a man possessed when it came to his computer. He seemed to think the machine had all the answers. Jose didn't agree. He knew how to use a computer, too, but to him it was just another tool.

Half an hour later they reached the Van Duzer Corridor, a federally protected stretch of forest. Jose rolled down his window and took a deep breath. "Man, smell all that green!" cried Jose. Looking out the windshield, he admired the giant firs and alders that covered the hills for as far as his eyes could see.

"Yeah, green," mumbled Hudson without taking his eyes off of his computer screen.

"You know, *amigo*, when I came up here from Mexico, I couldn't get over the trees. I'd never seen so many giant trees in all my life. I felt small in comparison," said Jose, a touch of awe in his voice.

"You *are* small," teased Hudson.

"No way. I'm *average*," retorted Jose. "I read it in a magazine. My height of five feet, eight inches is average. Not everyone is six feet like you. It's probably due to the rain."

"What are you talking about?" asked Hudson. The strangeness of Jose's remark made him look up from his computer.

"The rain made you grow tall, Hudson. Me, I grew up in a desert. With so little rain, my growth was stunted," said Jose, his brown eyes dancing with laughter.

"That's a bunch of hogwash if I ever heard it. You know that a person's height is determined genetically," stated Hudson matter-of-factly.

Jose grinned. "Ha! Sort of luck of the draw, right?"

"Exactly," answered Hudson.

"Well, it's no big deal. The *señoritas* like me anyway."

"When you start college this fall you'd better major in something besides girls," advised Hudson, rolling his eyes.

"You know, you could learn plenty from me about girls," teased Jose.

"I doubt that." Hudson turned his attention back to his computer screen.

An amused expression spread across Jose's face as he glanced sideways at his friend. He enjoyed their habit of teasing each other. It was an important part of their friendship.

The scenery gradually changed from lush woodlands to flat pasture land. Occasionally, a weatherbeaten house or rusted mobile home could be seen. The air coming in the pickup's window changed, too. Now it was damp and smelled of the sea.

They reached Grande Junction, a tiny fork in the road consisting of a gas station and a roadside diner. Jose turned left on the road leading to

Oregon's northern coast. On his left Jose could see a rushing stream working its way out to the sea.

"Have you ever been to Nescola?" Jose asked.

"No. I haven't been down to the coast since I was a kid," answered Hudson. He switched off his computer and stared out the window, eager to get his first glimpse of the sea.

"Nescola isn't much of a town. Just a cafe, a general store, a motel, and a golf course. Basically, it's a summer community of privately owned homes," explained Jose. Then a white stretch of beach and surf came into view, and Jose signaled a left turn.

"Well, why are we turning in here, then?" asked Hudson.

Jose was already crossing the highway toward a dirt road that was more like a path. Blackberry vines grabbed at the truck's sides as it bounced along the bumpy road.

"Well, your Aunt Dot didn't buy in Nescola, exactly. The house is on South Beach." Jose kept his eyes on the narrow road as he drove through the jungle of vines and overgrown shrubs.

"And why is that?" asked Hudson.

"The house was real cheap—I mean *real* cheap." Jose avoided the look in Hudson's eyes.

"All the places she buys are cheap. So what are you trying to say? Is this house more of a tumbledown shack than the usual?" Hudson asked. He wondered why Jose was suddenly acting so strangely.

"Nah, the house isn't too bad. Nothing we can't handle."

"So why did she get it so cheap?"

As the pickup rumbled along, Jose glanced sideways and decided to tell his friend the truth. "Some folks say it's haunted," he said quietly.

Chapter 2

Standing on the lawn, Hudson and Jose stared up at the old two-story house. The place had a wide porch with a row of windows and glass doors facing the sea. It looked weather-beaten and very run-down. "It's going to take more than a summer to fix up this place. It could take a week or more just to clear a path to the front door," groaned Hudson.

"All it needs is another layer of shingles on the roof and some fresh paint inside and out. Then it will look as good as new."

"Now I know why my aunt calls you an optimist," laughed Hudson, starting for the door.

Jose followed Hudson up the stone

steps. "So tell me—are you ready to meet the ghost?"

"I don't believe in ghosts," retorted Hudson. But as he stepped through the back door, he felt his heart race. The floorboards creaked eerily as he walked through the kitchen into the large living room.

Two old chairs and a sagging sofa sat in front of the stone fireplace. A thick layer of dust covered everything.

Jose popped his head into the back bedroom and bath. "We can bunk in here or in the living room," he said, returning to stand by Hudson at the windows facing the sea.

"You can see that this end of the beach is really isolated," Hudson said, looking southward at the arm of rocky cliffs that jutted into the water. "It must be at least a mile or more over to North Beach."

"That's not all *that* far to run if a ghost is chasing you," teased Jose, his eyes dancing with fun and merriment.

"Will you get off it, man? I stopped believing in ghosts when I was five," snapped Hudson as he stomped up the stairs. Entering a large room, he felt a rush of cold air. He checked the windows, but they were all closed. Glancing around, he saw that the room was empty except for a wooden rocker near the window overlooking the ocean.

"*Brrr*. It's cold up here," said Jose as he rounded the top of the stairs.

"Yeah."

"What a barn this big room is! Your Aunt Dot wants us to insulate the walls before we paint. But I think we should put up some walls and make three separate bedrooms," said Jose, starting back down the stairs.

"It would be a shame to divide up such a nice big space," said Hudson.

"Why? If you have guests you want them to have some privacy," said Jose. He remembered sharing a bedroom with his six brothers when he was a child. Hudson had been an only child. He had no idea what it was like to have no space to call your own.

"You have a point," agreed Hudson, thinking to himself that the inside rooms would no longer have a view of the ocean.

After unloading the truck, the boys spent a couple of hours cleaning the downstairs. Hudson threw open the French doors. He was about to step out on the porch when Jose stopped him.

"Some of the floorboards are rotten, *amigo*. I wouldn't want you to end up in the basement," chuckled Jose.

"Basement?" Hudson gave Jose a questioning look.

"Yeah. Outside, there's a door that leads down to the basement," explained Jose. "Come on, I'll show you."

The basement was dark and musty. Like a silent monster, an old coal-burning furnace sat in the middle of the room. Jose flipped open the firebox of the furnace. It was empty.

Hudson pointed to a pile of coal nearby. "Should we fire it up? Might take some of the chill off upstairs."

"I don't think we should chance it. We might burn the place down," explained Jose, closing the firebox door. The metal door clanged loudly in the quiet room. "After we get all this junk cleaned out, I'll get someone to check it out and make sure it works."

Tall stacks of dusty magazines, old newspapers, and broken beach chairs spilled from the dark corners. Hudson also noticed a standing mirror and a steamer trunk. He wondered what else lay hidden in the darkness.

Jose closed the basement door, then slapped Hudson on the back. "You know, *amigo*, I'm so hungry I could eat a bear. How about we go out and try that cafe in town?"

As they drove away, Hudson shifted

in his seat and glanced back at the house. He thought he saw movement in the upstairs window. Blinking, he had a creepy feeling that someone was watching them. When he looked again, nothing at all was moving. There was only the late afternoon sun glowing blood-red against the windows.

Chapter 3

Jose drove slowly through the narrow streets of Nescola. Beach houses of all styles lined the streets like a row of boxes. Finally they drove past a golf course, a long stretch of green dotted with a few scrubby trees.

"You ever play golf?" asked Jose, slowing for two golfers who were crossing the dirt road.

Hudson nodded.

"You like it?" asked Jose, his dark eyes wide with surprise. He couldn't picture Hudson playing any sport. Hudson was such a *mental* person, always working on his computer or reading a book.

"Yeah. It's fun. I like hitting the ball and watching it soar into the sky," answered Hudson, glancing at the small gray-shingled building that looked more like a tool shed than a clubhouse.

"Sounds like baseball. Me, I *love* baseball," said Jose. Then he slowed the pickup to inch past the horse stable, where several young women were unsaddling horses. As he cruised by, he turned for another look.

Noticing the intense focus of Jose's attention, Hudson laughed. "I'd say that girl-watching is your sport."

Jose shrugged and shot another glance in the rearview mirror before turning the corner. "How am I going to find my true love if I don't look?"

As they headed toward the Nescola Cafe, a pretty dark-haired girl of about seventeen walked by. Jose greeted her and got her talking. Within seconds, he had learned her name, her address, and the fact that she was spending the summer in Nescola with her family. Hudson shifted his weight nervously and looked down at his shoes while Jose and the girl talked.

Finally, smiling at Jose and giving Hudson a little wave, she said good-bye.

Jose clapped Hudson on the back as they entered the cafe. "Maybe she has a friend."

Hudson pulled away, suddenly irritable. "Look, don't go trying to fix me up, okay?"

"I was just kidding. What's wrong with you?" asked Jose, pulling out a chair at a small table.

Hudson reached for a menu. "I didn't come down here to have a good time. The sooner we get that ratty old house fixed up, the sooner we can get back to Portland."

"Oh, lighten up, Hud. There are only so many working hours in the day. No law says that we can't enjoy ourselves while we're here," said Jose. Out of the corner of his eye, he glanced toward the general store where the girl, Merrilee, had disappeared just a few moments before.

Hudson noticed his glance and frowned again. Jose was right. They couldn't work every minute. But the idea of meeting new girls made his stomach knot with fear. Secretly he admired Jose's easy, friendly manner with girls. He wished he could be more cool and relaxed, but he couldn't. Something inside him would just freeze up whenever a girl even looked in his direction.

Jose changed the subject back to the house and what they had to do. They ordered burgers, fries, and sodas with apple pie for dessert.

After dinner, they bought groceries at the general store and headed back to the house. It was already dark when they drove down the dirt road toward the house. Again, the sounds of overgrown branches scratching the sides of the pickup echoed in the cab.

When they parked, Jose pulled out a flashlight. He played the light across the damp ground and up the steps, making it easier for them to see where they were going.

"First thing tomorrow, I'm cutting down these bushes," grumbled Hudson. "I'm getting tired of being clawed and scratched."

"Replacing the broken light bulb on the garage will help, too," added Jose. The absolute darkness of the place made him uneasy.

"You're not scared, are you?" teased Hudson, hearing something in his friend's voice that he hadn't heard before.

"Naw. I just don't want to break my leg or something," lied Jose. At the back door, he reached in and flipped on the kitchen light. Then he checked each room, making sure no one had come in while they were gone.

"When I came down here with Dot, I offered to get new locks. But she said that no one locks their doors around here," Jose called out to Hudson, who was putting away groceries.

"Dot is still living in the sixties," grumbled Hudson, striding up the stairs two at a time. He flipped on the upstairs light. Nothing had changed. The rocker still sat by the window. Retracing his steps, he stopped at the landing and studied the old grandfather clock. The clock's hands read three o'clock. The pendulum was still.

"I wonder if this old thing works?" said Hudson, talking more to himself than to Jose. Opening the glass doors of the clock, he found the key. He wound the clock and then set the hands to read eight o'clock. Nothing happened. But when he gave the pendulum a push, it began to swing.

"Got it working, huh?" Jose watched the pendulum swing back and forth.

"It just needed winding," said Hudson, closing the glass doors.

Jose shook his head as he listened to the tick-tocking of the clock. "That is a *loud* clock, man. They can probably hear it over on North Beach."

"The sound should go nicely with your snoring," teased Hudson.

Jose made a fire to chase away the damp chill while Hudson laid out their sleeping bags. They sat talking until the grandfather clock chimed eleven. Jose yawned. "I think I'll turn in. Get an early start tomorrow."

Hudson stretched and stood up. "Good idea. I'll get the lights." He circled through the downstairs rooms, turning off the lights, then climbed into his sleeping bag. The house was dark except for the last flickerings of the fire that sent shadows slithering up the wall. Outside, the surf pounded against the beach. Hudson glanced over at Jose and saw that he was already asleep.

Hudson lay on his back and stared up at the ceiling. He listened to the ticking of the clock and the creaking of the old house. He wondered who had started the story about the house being haunted. *Probably just a campfire story*, he told himself as he snuggled deeper into his bag.

Late in the night, the sound of a door banging woke Hudson from his sleep. Startled, he sat up and saw that Jose was sleeping like a baby. Hudson shivered. The French doors were wide open! Cold sea air poured into the room. *That's strange*, he thought, getting up to close the doors.

He looked outside. There was no wind. The tall firs and the bushes surrounding the front yard were still.

Shivering, Hudson hurried back to his sleeping bag. He glanced at the grandfather clock. It had stopped working. It read three o'clock.

Chapter 4

It must be a hundred degrees up here! thought Hudson as he put down his hammer and wiped the sweat from his forehead. He squinted at the blue sky. Not a cloud in sight. No relief from the burning sun. Sitting down next to a pile of shingles, he gazed out at the ocean. From his position on the roof, he could see the coastline curving northward. On North Beach, children and families looked like dots of color. He watched as a dog retrieved a stick and ran back to his master.

"Work getting to be too much for you, old buddy?" teased Jose, squatting down next to Hudson.

"We've been at this roof for a week now. Can't a man take a break?"

grumbled Hudson. Not really upset, he was finding that he actually liked pushing himself to the limit.

"We should finish by this afternoon, *if* you ever get back to work." Jose grinned broadly and crossed to the lower part of the roof where he'd been working. "Then you can get back to tinkering with that clock of yours."

Hudson shook his head and picked up his hammer. He shouldn't have told Jose about finding the French doors open that first night. Jose had gone on and on about ghosts. *Well, he's wrong*, thought Hudson, nailing a shingle into place. *The doors probably weren't shut properly to begin with. And the clock— well, it probably just needs some new springs and the hands fixed.* He planned to test it that night.

They had just nailed the last shingle in place when Hudson heard girls' voices. He glanced at Jose, who winked at him. "I think we have company."

Hudson groaned.

"Hey, Merrilee!" Jose called out. "Who's that with you?"

"This is my friend, Annie James. Come on down and meet her," Merrilee yelled back.

Jose gathered up the remaining shingles and started down the ladder. He stopped and looked back up at Hudson, who was staring out at the ocean. "Come on, Hud. You can't avoid girls all your life."

Hudson followed, frowning. "I'm not trying to avoid anyone," he hissed in a low whisper when they reached the ground. "I just don't have anything to say."

Jose grinned. "I'm sure you'll think of something. So what do you girls think of the roof?"

"It looks great. We could see you two working up there from over at North Beach," answered Merrilee. She smiled and turned to her friend.

"Annie's grandmother owns the stable. Annie knows everything about horses."

"Well, I don't know *everything*," Annie said shyly. "I just know how to ride and take care of them."

"You're too modest. She's going to be a veterinarian," announced Merrilee with obvious pride in her friend. Then she turned and smiled at Jose. "Want to go swimming?"

Jose glanced at Hudson, who was studying the tops of his sneakers like he'd never seen them before. "Sounds like a plan. The roof is finished. No use starting another project this late in the day. What do you say, Hudson?"

"Sure, I could go for a swim. I was sweating bullets up there."

"I feel that way sometimes when I ride my horse in the middle of the day. The sun feels like it's burning right through my skin," Annie said, giving him a sweet smile.

Hudson liked her immediately. He

gave her a small, shy grin.

"So what are we waiting for? Let's get our suits on," said Jose, slapping Hudson on the back as he turned to go into the house.

Within minutes, they rejoined the girls. The four of them trooped across the dunes and down to the flat sand. Jose spread a blanket on the sand. They dropped their T-shirts on the blanket, then ran down to the ocean. When the first wave broke against their legs, they screamed and yelled at the coldness of the water. Soon they were swimming and splashing each other.

Hudson and Annie were the first to return to the blanket. They both grabbed towels and quickly dried themselves. "The water felt good," grinned Hudson, "but this towel feels even better." He wrapped the towel around his shoulders and flopped down in the warm sand.

"I know what you mean," laughed

Annie, drying her long blond hair with her towel.

Annie sat down next to him and again she smiled. Her blue eyes seemed to reflect the blue of the sky and the sea. Suddenly shy again, Hudson looked away from her, trying to think of something to say.

Merrilee and Jose ran up and threw themselves on the blanket. Jose shook his head like a wet dog. Tiny drops of water flew everywhere.

"Hey, watch it, Jose!" yelled Hudson, wiping the water from his face and arms.

Jose laughed. "Thought I'd cool you off, man. Say, Annie, did Hudson tell you about the ghost?"

"Ghost?" asked Merrilee, her brown eyes wide with curiosity.

"No, he didn't," answered Annie, looking first at Jose, then Hudson. "Did you guys really see a ghost? My grandmother told me that the house you're working on is haunted, but I never really believed her."

Hudson frowned at Jose. "I didn't really see a ghost," he explained. "The first night we were here, the French doors blew open and the grandfather clock stopped ticking. Coincidences, nothing more. It's my friend Jose here who's so afraid of things that go bump in the night."

Jose threw up his hands in a kind of defense. "I never said I was afraid of ghosts! I just said I believe they exist."

"I do, too," added Merrilee in an excited whisper. "I mean, where would ghost stories come from if *someone* hadn't seen a ghost?"

Annie laughed. "Oh, Merrilee! Don't you know that ghost stories come from people's imaginations?"

"Right," agreed Hudson. "There's no such things as ghosts and goblins."

"Then explain to us why everyone thinks your Aunt Dot's beach house is haunted," challenged Jose, glancing back at the strange old house that seemed to loom over them.

"I know why people think it's haunted," piped up Annie.

They all turned and looked at her. Smiling shyly at the attention, she continued. "It's because the original owner hung himself in there."

Everyone stared at Annie as she went on.

"My grandmother said that years ago, a Mr. Bailey built the house for his wife and three daughters. They spent their summers here. Then one summer the poor mother and her three little daughters were playing in the ocean when they were swept out to sea. The man saw the waves suck them out. He tried to save them, but it was too late.

"Their bodies were never found. Grandmother said the man spent the rest of the summer staring out at the ocean. People could see him sitting in a rocker on the second floor. He just went crazy with grief. Hung himself over there," said Annie. She pointed toward the rocky cliffs that jutted into the sea at the end of South Beach.

"Wow, that's *spooky*," whispered Merrilee with a little shiver.

"So now he waits in the house for their return," added Jose, thoughtfully.

"Oh, come on," snapped Hudson in disgust. "It's a sad story, but that's all it is. No one is waiting in the house— except maybe a few mice." But a few moments later, glancing back at the old house, he thought he saw movement in the upstairs window. Just like he'd seen the day they had arrived.

Chapter 5

After a dinner of franks and beans, Hudson reassembled the grandfather clock. Then he wound it and set the pendulum to swinging.

Jose came over and stood next to him. "How is it working now?"

"Perfectly," answered Hudson. "The parts just needed oiling and some adjustments. I don't think it will be stopping again—unless I forget to wind it every day."

Jose eyed the clock suspiciously. Then he gave Hudson a teasing look. "Or unless the ghost upstairs starts messing with it."

Hudson flashed Jose a disgusted look. "Yeah, *right!*"

With a raised eyebrow, Jose added,

"I guess we'll see at three o'clock tonight, won't we?"

"I'm not staying up to find out," snapped Hudson. "*You* can if you want, but I'm bushed." He crossed to the old sofa and picked up his sleeping bag, unrolling it in front of the fire. Then he sat down, staring at the flames.

Jose flopped down on the sofa. "You shouldn't dismiss the idea of ghosts so quickly, Hud. In every culture there are stories about ghosts and spirits. So there *must* be something behind all those stories."

"There's no scientific evidence to prove that ghosts exist. It's like Annie said—they're just stories told to frighten people. I suppose you believe in fairy-tales, too," snorted Hudson.

"No, but I believe in spirits. When I was growing up in Mexico I heard many stories of hauntings and spirits. People swore they had seen ghosts. Sure, some of the stories were too fantastic to believe. But others . . . well, they had some elements of truth to them. And how do you explain away something that hundreds of people have seen?" argued Jose.

"Like what?" asked Hudson, lying on his side and staring up at Jose.

"Like *La Loba*, the wolf woman," said Jose, his expression serious as he stared into the fire.

Hudson smiled, knowing he was in for one of Jose's tall tales. "Okay, so who is *La Loba*?"

"*La Loba* is a wolf woman. She is a collector of bones who lives in a hidden cave. But many have seen her. Some have seen her driving in a burnt-out car. Others have spotted her standing by the road near El Paso. Truckers have said she rode shotgun with them to Morelia, Mexico. Still others have seen her walking in the hills above Oaxaca with firewood on her back.

"But always she is collecting bones,

bones of the wolf. She crawls through the mountains, arroyos, and dry riverbeds, searching for bones. When she has collected all the bones of a wolf, she stands over the skeleton and sings the creature back to life. They say she does this for many animals that are in danger of becoming extinct."

"That sounds like a myth to me—a folktale," argued Hudson, grinning.

"But *so many* people have seen her! They also say that she has saved many a person who was lost in the desert," Jose added firmly.

Hudson plumped up his pillow. He gave Jose an amused nod. "Okay, okay. If I'm ever lost in the desert I will certainly look for *La Loba*."

"You do that, *amigo*," said Jose. "She may save your life."

"Or maybe she'll pick my bones clean," teased Hudson.

"No, your kind is not in danger of becoming extinct," laughed Jose. He slipped into his sleeping bag and made himself comfortable. "Wake me if the ghost starts prowling the house."

Hudson shook his head and laughed. Then he, too, snuggled down into his bag. He was tired from working all day in the hot sun. He thought about Annie and smiled to himself. He liked her. She was pretty and smart and easy to talk to. He closed his eyes and soon felt sleep pulling all thoughts from his mind.

Sometime in the middle of the night, a rhythmic rocking sound awoke Hudson. Startled, he sat up. Cold air swept in around his shoulders. He shivered. *A window or door must be open*, he thought. He squinted in the darkness in the direction of the French doors, but they were closed. He listened for the sound that had awakened him but heard only the howling of the wind. After several minutes, he got up and fumbled for the table lamp. Jose stirred in his sleep and opened his eyes.

"What's going on, man?" asked Jose, his voice grouchy with sleep.

"I heard a noise and then I felt this cold draft on me," explained Hudson, pulling his sweatshirt on. "Probably a window or door has come open. I'm just going to check."

"It is the ghost, *amigo*," said Jose, a worried expression spreading across his face. Slowly, he crawled out of his bag. He stretched and reached for his shirt. *"Brrrr!* It's colder than a freezer in here, Hud. What's going on?"

Hudson crossed to the kitchen, switching lights on as he went. He checked the back door and the kitchen windows. They were all closed. Coming back into the living room, he saw Jose coming out of the back bedroom.

"There's nothing open back there," yawned Jose.

Hudson walked over to the stairs, thinking he would check the second floor. He glanced at the grandfather clock as he went by. Then he turned and walked back to it. Again, the clock had stopped at exactly three o'clock. Hudson looked at his wristwatch. It read three fifteen.

Jose was staring at the clock, too. His eyes were wide with apprehension. "I thought you fixed the clock!"

"I did." Hudson couldn't explain why it had stopped again—and at the same time it had stopped before. Glancing at the ceiling, he felt a sense of dread come over him. For some unexplainable reason, he didn't want to go up there. Finally he forced himself to walk up the stairs.

Jose followed close behind. "I don't like this, *amigo*. I have a bad feeling."

"Will you stop it!" snapped Hudson. Flipping on the upstairs wall switch, he looked toward the back of the room, but couldn't see anything. But the front windows were all wide open. "Look!

There's the problem," Hudson said.

Together, they quickly latched the windows shut. "There's no way these windows just came open by themselves. It *must* have been the ghost," whispered Jose fearfully.

Hudson played with the old locks that kept the windows shut. "These latches are awfully old. The wind probably blew them open."

"Yeah, maybe." Jose frowned.

Passing behind the rocking chair, Jose gave it a push. The rocker moved back and forth, making a loud, rhythmic rocking sound on the old wooden floor.

Hudson spun around and stared. His sunburned face was as white as a sheet. It was the same sound that had startled him awake.

Chapter 6

When Jose woke up, he found Hudson sitting in front of his laptop computer. "What are you doing up so early?" he asked.

Hudson glanced at his friend. "A little detective work on your ghost, Mr. Scaredy Pants."

"So now he's *my* ghost?" laughed Jose, pulling his jeans on.

Hudson walked over to the old grandfather clock. "Last night, the sound that woke me was the sound of the rocker rocking. And the clock stopped exactly at three o'clock again. I can't explain it."

Jose's eyes widened. "That's more than a coincidence, *amigo*. That's *proof* that there's a ghost in this house."

"Don't go jumping to conclusions," frowned Hudson.

"What else can I think?" asked Jose, glancing at the ceiling, wondering if the ghost was upstairs that very minute.

"*Seeing* the ghost would be proof," answered Hudson. "Anyway, since I couldn't sleep, I decided to find out a little more about this Mr. Bailey. First I checked the state's property records and found the original land deed. It stated that a Mr. William Bailey bought the land in 1933. Then I plugged into the newspaper archive and looked at all the old articles about accidents in the late 1930s."

"What did you find?"

"I found a short article about a Mrs. Bailey and her three daughters. It said they were swept out to sea by a rip tide. So that part of Annie's story checks out," Hudson explained.

"Did you find anything about Bailey

hanging himself?" asked Jose.

Hudson shook his head. "That's what seems so strange. I couldn't find anything about the hanging—or even Mr. Bailey's obituary."

Shrugging, Jose started for the kitchen. "His family probably covered it up. You know how squeamish people are about suicides."

"Yeah," agreed Hudson, following him into the kitchen.

Gulping milk from the carton, Jose grinned. "So, we've got ourselves a ghost. You think he hung himself at three o'clock?"

"How would I know?" snapped Hudson. He poured himself a bowl of cereal and reached for the milk carton Jose was holding. "You *could* use a glass, you know."

"Then I'd have to wash it," laughed Jose. Seeing Hudson's sour expression, he became serious. "Look, you like to think everything in life is supposed to be logical. Neat, tidy explanations. But spirits and ghosts defy logic."

"Which is why they don't exist," mumbled Hudson, his mouth full of cereal. "Let's forget the ghost. What are we doing today?"

"Painting the outside. Best to do it while the weather is still nice. Dot wants the outside to be gray with white trim, just like it was originally."

After covering all the windows with paper, they hooked up a sprayer and began painting the house. As the day wore on, the temperature rose. Rivers of sweat ran down their faces and soaked their shirts. But they didn't stop until they had finished painting the sides and back areas of the house.

When they were done, Jose turned on the garden hose and doused his face and head with water. Hudson went into the kitchen for some cold sodas. Returning, he handed one to Jose.

"It's looking good," said Hudson,

admiring their work. "Once we get the trim painted it will look like it did back when it was built," said Jose, studying the house.

"I wonder if your ghost, Mr. Bailey, will be happy then?" teased Hudson, finishing the last of his soda.

Jose laughed. "He's *your* ghost. You're the one who heard him rocking upstairs. I'll tell you what. I'm going to think of a way for us to catch sight of the ghost." Jose's expression was serious with thought.

Hudson laughed. "What are you going to do? Call Ghostbusters?"

Jose chuckled. "Don't you worry. I'll think of something."

Chapter 7

By the end of the week, the outside painting was finished. The white trim looked bright and shiny against the gray front and sides.

But Jose still hadn't come up with a plan to catch the ghost. Every night they heard the rocking sound upstairs. And every night the clock continued to stop at three o'clock.

One night Jose had run up the stairs, hoping to catch sight of the ghost. A couple of times they saw the rocker moving ever so slowly back and forth—as if someone had just gotten up. Jose insisted that the moving chair proved the existence of the ghost. But Hudson didn't agree. He argued that the wind could have set it in motion.

On Saturday morning they replaced the rotten planks on the porch. When they were done, Jose stretched and gave Hudson a sly smile. "Listen up. I think I know how we can catch a glimpse of our ghost."

"How?" asked Hudson, following him to the backyard.

"You'll see," answered Jose, his eyes dancing as he opened the basement door and flicked on the light.

Hudson followed him down into the dimly lit room. Then he watched as Jose began pulling junk from the musty corners.

"Come on, *amigo*. Don't just stand there. Start hauling this stuff outside so we can get rid of it," commanded Jose, shoving a pile of broken beach chairs toward his friend.

Hudson groaned. He wanted to take the afternoon off and spend some time on the beach. "I thought we were going swimming. Work on our tans."

Jose laughed. *"Tan?* You're red as a lobster. Now quit complaining and come help me."

Hudson agreed. He really didn't need any more sun. His skin was burned and beginning to peel. He grabbed an armload of old chairs and headed up the stairs.

They worked steadily for over an hour, dragging newspapers, tools, cola bottles, moldy wicker furniture, and a steamer trunk out to the yard.

Hudson tried to open the trunk, but it was locked. Sifting through the box of tools, he found a screwdriver and a hammer. Using the screwdriver as a wedge, he hammered it beneath the round lock. Finally the lock flew open, and he lifted the trunk's lid. Folded neatly inside were piles of women's and girls' summer clothes. *These must have belonged to the wife and little girls,* thought Hudson.

"Jose, come look at this stuff,"

Hudson said. When he got no answer, he turned around. Jose was gone. "Jose!" he called out in a louder voice.

"I'll be there in a minute," Jose yelled back, his voice drifting up from the basement.

Gently, Hudson lifted the clothes from the trunk and laid them on the ground. A sadness swept through him as he picked up three small dolls. In his mind, he could picture the girls laughing and playing on the beach with their dolls. When he imagined them being swept out to sea with their mother, he shuddered.

"What's wrong, Hud?" asked Jose, appearing in the doorway. He was half-carrying, half-dragging an antique standing mirror. He righted the mirror on its legs and then crossed over and squatted down next to Hudson.

"Looking at all of this stuff, I guess I just started feeling bad," explained Hudson, indicating the clothes and the three old dolls from the steamer trunk.

Jose nodded. He could understand what his friend was feeling. He remembered when his father had died —how the clothes in his father's closet had seemed so lifeless. A lump came to his throat like it did whenever he thought of his father. He shook his head and stared up at the sky. It was filled with gray clouds, heavy with rain.

"Hey, look at this." Hudson held up a faded photograph. "It must be Mrs. Bailey and her girls." He glanced at the back of the photo. Someone had written *Nescola beach, 1935.*

Jose looked at the picture. The woman and her three small daughters were blond and pretty. Dressed alike in sailor dresses, they smiled for the camera. "Nice-looking family," said Jose. He started to place the photo back in the trunk, then thought better of it. Carefully, he stuck it in the pocket of his T-shirt. *This might come in handy later on*, he thought to himself.

Then Hudson lifted a small, wooden jewelry box from the trunk. At the same moment, he felt a drop of rain on his arm.

Jose felt it, too. "Looks like it's going to really pour in a minute. Let's get this stuff back in the trunk." Hudson agreed, and they quickly returned the items to the trunk and closed the lid. Carrying the jewelry box under his arm, Hudson started for the house.

"Wait. I need you to help me get this mirror inside," said Jose.

"Why do you want that cracked old thing?" asked Hudson.

"You'll see," answered Jose as they hauled it into the house.

Chapter 8

Sometime after seven o'clock, the phone rang. It was Annie and Merrilee inviting the boys to a movie. Holding his hand over the receiver, Hudson asked Jose if he wanted to go.

"Maybe tomorrow. Tonight we've got a date with a ghost," answered Jose with a sly smile.

Hudson could tell that Jose had made up his mind. He knew that he couldn't argue his friend out of it. He felt his spirits sink. He liked Annie and wanted to see her again. But now he would have to wait. Quickly, he explained to her what they were up to. Glancing out the window, he saw the rain whipping the trees. "We'll take a raincheck," he joked.

Noticing the disappointment on Hudson's face, Jose couldn't resist teasing him a bit. "I think you've been bitten by the love bug, *amigo*."

"I like Annie. She's easy to talk to. But it's no big deal," he snapped. Wanting to change the subject, he picked up the jewelry box he had taken from the trunk.

"You think there's anything valuable in there?" Jose asked.

"We'll see." The lock opened easily. Inside was an assortment of costume jewelry. Raking his fingers through the beads and fake jewels, Hudson felt something on the bottom of the box. Carefully, he lifted out a letter. The paper was faded with age. He stared at the envelope. It was addressed to a Lucinda Sherman.

"Read it," Jose said eagerly.

Hudson opened the envelope. Inside was an old-fashioned valentine. He glanced at the sentiment, then looked at what had been written. "To my dearest love. I know that your parents want you to wait a year before marrying me. Don't worry. I would wait a lifetime for you. I love you deeply. You are my life. William Bailey." Hudson slipped the letter back in its envelope.

Jose was quiet for a moment. When he spoke, his voice was heavy with emotion. "Wow. He really loved her. No wonder he went crazy with grief when she and his girls were drowned."

Hudson stared at the blazing fire. Jose reached over and took the letter. He stuck it in his pocket with the photograph he'd taken from the trunk.

"What are you going to do with the letter?" asked Hudson.

"You'll see," replied Jose, glancing at the clock, which was ticking off the hours. "I see you fixed the clock again."

"Yeah," smiled Hudson. "For some reason it bothers me when it stops."

Jose raised an eyebrow, but he

didn't comment. Instead, he asked Hudson to help him carry the antique mirror upstairs.

"Why?"

Jose gave him an exasperated look. "So we can catch a glimpse of ghost."

"What makes you think we'll see his reflection when we haven't seen him rocking in the chair?" asked Hudson.

"Remember that story I told you about *La Loba*, the wolf woman? Well, the truckers said they saw *La Loba* in their side mirror, sitting in the passenger seat. But not one ever saw her by just looking *directly at* her."

As they reached the top of the stairs, Jose flipped on the light. They stood the old mirror on its feet, then angled it toward the rocker. Jose pointed to the wall near the stairs. "If we sit over there, we'll be able to see the ghost in the mirror when it sits in the rocker."

Hudson shook his head. "This is

crazy. I'm not going to sit up here and wait all night for a ghost!"

Jose grinned. "Too scary for you?"

"No!" snapped Hudson. "I'll stay here all right—but I'm just telling you it's a waste of time."

"We'll see," answered Jose. He took the photograph and letter and laid them on the seat of the rocker. Then he crossed to the wall near the stairs and sat down next to Hudson.

"What did you do that for?" asked Hudson, pointing to the photo and the folded letter.

"I thought our ghost, Mr. Bailey, might like to have them. Perhaps those things will give him some comfort," whispered Jose.

Hudson rolled his eyes. He leaned back against the wall to wait.

Lost in their thoughts, the boys sat silently. Sometime around midnight, both of them fell asleep. When the grandfather clock chimed two o'clock,

Hudson jerked awake. He glanced at Jose, who was snoring lightly. He gave him a couple of jabs to wake him up.

"What?" asked Jose, sleepily.

"It's two o'clock. Another hour and your ghost will be here," whispered Hudson.

Jose yawned. "Thanks." He glanced at the rocker. It wasn't moving. He shivered. "It's getting colder up here, don't you think?"

Hudson thought the room had grown colder, too. "It's the storm. The wind is seeping in through the cracks in the walls," he explained, glad to have a logical explanation.

Jose started to say something, but he stopped. *The rocker had begun to move!* He nudged Hudson in the ribs.

"I see it," whispered Hudson. His heart was racing. He couldn't believe his eyes. The empty rocker was slowly moving back and forth. Jose, his eyes wide as plates, gestured with his head

that they should look in the mirror.

Slowly, they turned their eyes back to the rocker. The rocking motion was getting faster. Hudson shifted his eyes toward the old mirror and gasped. Reflected in the mirror was a man sitting in the rocker. He was dressed in an old-fashioned black suit. A coiled rope lay on his lap. He was holding the photograph and the valentine that Jose had placed there.

As they watched, the ghostly figure stood up. Leaving the rope on the rocker, he smiled and took a step in their direction.

Barely breathing, both Hudson and Jose shrank back against the wall. They couldn't see the ghost reflected in the mirror now. The angle was wrong. But they felt a coldness sweep by them. "He's going to hang himself again," whispered Jose.

Hudson hugged himself. He had

never felt so cold. "No, I don't think so." He nodded toward the rope on the rocker's seat. "I think he's finally going to join his wife and daughters."

"So do you believe in ghosts *now?*" asked Jose.

"Yes," whispered Hudson, staring at the empty rocker.

Downstairs, the grandfather clock chimed three o'clock.